THIS BOOK BELONGS TO:

Who's There?

Let's knock and see!

Written and Illustrated by
Donna Sven and Art Intell

Knock, knock, what's behind the door? Open it up to see what's in store! A friendly bear or a smiling sun, Every door hides a world of fun!

Knock on the door and see who's near.

It's a frog filled with cheer!

Knock, knock, who's come to call?

It is a sloth who's not in a hurry at all.

◇

Turn the page, take a peek,

It's a parrot who loves to speak!

Knock, knock, who has come today?

Is it a dolphin in the bay?

Turn the page, what a sight.

It's a unicorn glowing bright!

◇

Knock on the door, who's come to play?

It is a peacock bright as day?

———————◇———————

Knock, knock, what's the sound?

Is it a cat that's prowling around?

◇

Turn the page, what a sight,

It's an owl, gliding through the night!

◇

Turn the page, what's the fun?

It's a dog, ready to run!

———————◇———————

We are at the end, what will we see?

Bye!

It's a zebra, waving back at me!

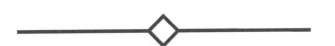

About The Author

Donna Sven is a children's book author from Long Island, New York. Donna's creative spirit was nurtured as a child, shaping her understanding of the world. She believes that creativity is not just an art but the pinnacle of knowledge. Through her stories, she aims to inspire young minds to dream beyond boundaries and embrace their own creative powers, fostering a generation that values imagination and innovation.

THE END

Made in the USA
Las Vegas, NV
12 December 2024

14058545R00031